Jacqueline Wilson

Illustrated by Georgien Overwater

For Brighid and Joe Reilly
and all their family

First published in Great Britain 1996
by Methuen Children's Books Ltd
Published 1997 by Mammoth
an imprint of Reed International Books Limited
Michelin House, 81 Fulham Road, London SW3 6RB

ISBN 0 7497 2826 4

10 9 8 7 6 5 4

A CIP catalogue record for this title
is available from the British Library

Printed in Great Britain
by Caledonian International Book Manufacturing Ltd, Glasgow

Contents

1 Swim Scare

'We're going swimming!' Connie sang happily.

'Sh!' said Dad. 'You'll wake the babies.'

Connie clamped her hand over her mouth, giggling. She certainly didn't want to wake her little brother and sister. They were called Claire and Charles and they were twins. They were both bald, with beady blue eyes, big tummies and bendy legs. Connie's gran said they were the most beautiful babies in the whole world. Connie thought Gran had gone a bit crackers. The twins looked *terrible*.

Their behaviour wasn't up to much either. They cried a lot during the day. They cried a lot during the night, too.

'Little monsters,' said Dad, yawning. 'They just wouldn't stop crying last night.'

'Tut, tut,' said Connie, shaking her head at the silly twins. '*They* won't be able to go swimming for years and years, will they, Dad?'

It seemed like years and years since Connie and Dad had gone swimming. Dad had been promising to take her for ages. But since the twins were born he was always too tired.

'*Next* Sunday,' he always said.

But now *this* Sunday he was really taking her.

'I love love *love* going swimming,' said Connie.

She made impressive sweeping movements with her arms, swimming through thin air.

'Look Dad! I can remember how to do it,' said Connie.

She 'swam' right out of the house, tiptoeing down the stairs and along the hall. Dad closed the front door very gently behind them.

He put his ear to the door and listened. 'Silence! The twins are still asleep. And so is

Mum. Lucky Mum.'

'Lucky *us*,' said Connie. 'We're going swimming.'

'Lucky us,' said Dad – but he didn't sound as if he meant it.

Connie practised her swimming strokes in the back of the car.

'Hey, stop kicking my seat!' said Dad.

'I'm doing my leg movements,' said Connie. 'Like a little frog. Just the way you showed me, Dad. I'm going to swim right up and down the little pool, you just wait and see.'

'Without keeping one foot on the bottom all the time?' said Dad, grinning.

'Cheek!' said Connie.

She got changed quickly in the cubicle at the swimming-bath. Her swimming costume was getting a bit small for her. Connie had to pull it down hard to make sure it covered her bottom properly. It had a blue dolphin on the front, with a big smily mouth. Connie gave him a little pat, her own mouth big and smily.

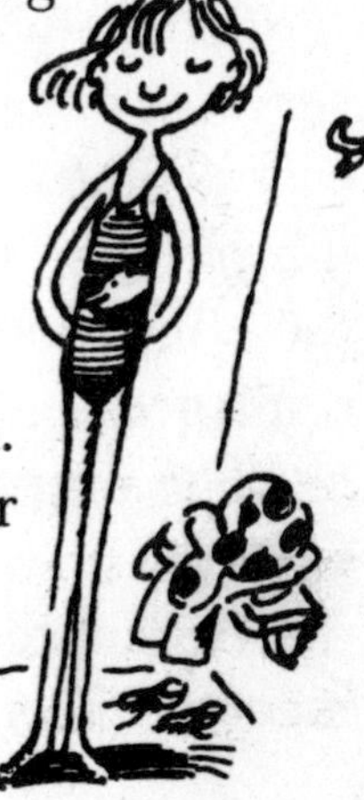

'I'm ready, Dad! Let's get in the little pool quick,' said

Connie.

But Connie and Dad found that the learner pool was roped off. There were lots of mums and a few dads and a lot of babies in the pool so Connie ducked under the rope ready to join them.

'No, dear, you can't come in here,' said the attendant. 'There's a parent-and-baby session taking place.'

'But we always go in the little pool,' said Connie. 'Dad's my parent.'

'She's my very big baby,' said Dad, joking.

'Much *too* big, I'm afraid,' said the attendant.

'Never mind, we'll go in the big pool,' said Dad. He took hold of Connie's hand. 'It'll be much more fun.'

Connie wasn't so sure. The big pool was very very big. The water got very deep and every fifteen minutes they switched the wave machine on. Huge waves rippled up and down the big pool and everyone shouted and screamed.

'The waves might knock me over, Dad,' said Connie.

'We'll keep to the edge when the wave machine is on,' said Dad. 'Come on, Connie.

Let's get in the water, eh?'

Dad went down the steps into the water. It came up to his waist. Connie went down the steps very slowly, one at a time. She would have stayed halfway down, but some bigger girls wanted to get in the water too.

'Move out of the way, you're blocking the steps,' they said, and when Connie didn't budge one of them pushed her.

It was only a little push, but Connie lost her grip on the handrail. She fell forward, screaming. She went splosh into the bright blue water. It closed over her head and she clawed and kicked in this new terrifying blue world. Then something grabbed hold of her. She was whirled upwards and her head burst out in the air, ears popping with the sudden noise.

'Poor old Connie! Were you trying to dive in?' said Dad.

Connie coughed and spluttered and clung to Dad. She put her arms tight round his neck and her legs tight round his waist, clinging to him like baby Charles or baby Claire.

'Hey! What's up? It's OK, you're not out of your depth here, Connie. This is the shallow end,' said Dad. 'Come on now, don't be such a baby.'

The girls who had pushed her were staring and giggling.

'Put your feet down on the bottom, Connie,' said Dad.

'I don't want to,' Connie said.

'Don't be silly now,' said Dad, and he pulled her legs down.

'No, no, don't, I'll go under!' said Connie, panicking.

'Of course you won't,' said Dad. 'There. See? You can stand up easily. Your whole head's out of the water.'

Connie stuck her chin up as high as it would go. The water lapped around her neck.

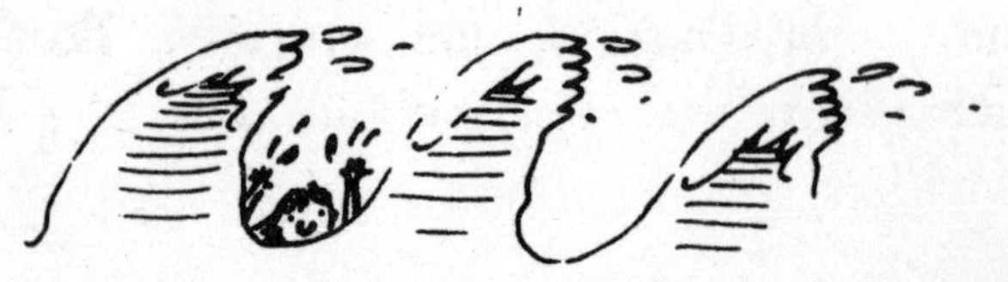

'I want to get out now,' said Connie.

'You've only just got in! I thought you were going to show me what a good swimmer you are.'

'I've changed my mind,' said Connie.

'Well, let's try one or two strokes, eh?' said Dad. 'I'll hold you up, don't worry. I'll put my hand under your chin, OK? I've got you. Just relax now.'

Connie didn't see how she could possibly relax when her eyes were stinging, her ears were popping, her throat was hurting, her swimming costume was digging right into her, lots of girls were laughing at her, Dad was starting to get cross, and she was in a huge enormous pool of water and could drown any minute.

But she did try one feeble little kick, one pathetic sweep of her arms. And then there was an announcement and a shriek of excitement and suddenly the water started tugging and heaving as if it was alive, a great water monster ready to gobble Connie up. They'd switched the wave machine on.

'I'm getting out!' said Connie, and she fought her way to the steps.

Dad was cross because they'd only had five minutes in the water and it was a waste of money. Connie didn't care. She knew one thing. She was never ever ever going swimming again.

2 Spaghetti Worms

'Coming swimming on Sunday?' said Dad.

'No fear,' Connie said.

Dad looked at Mum. Mum looked at Dad. They both looked at Connie.

'Why don't you give it another try, love?' said Mum.

'I don't like swimming now. I hate it.'

She stared at her plate. Mum had cooked spaghetti bolognese for tea, Connie's all-time favourite, for the first time since the twins were born. Mum hadn't had much time for proper cooking.

Claire and Charles had actually been very good for a while, cooing and kicking their legs. They'd started to get a bit niggly the moment Mum started serving up the spaghetti, but Dad had popped their dummies in place and they acted like stoppers.

Connie had been all set to enjoy her meal but now her tummy had gone tight at the very mention of swimming.

'I think it's time you learnt to swim properly,' said Dad. 'You were very *nearly* swimming before. Just a few lessons and you'll be bobbing about in the water, no bother.'

'I don't *want* to,' said Connie.

'I'll make sure you don't go under again, I promise,' said Dad.

'I know I'm not going to go under. Because I'm not going *in*,' said Connie.

She wound a portion of spaghetti round and round her fork. It was starting to look awfully like a lot of orange worms.

'Don't play with your food, darling. Eat it,' said Mum.

'I'm not very hungry any more,' said Connie, putting down her fork.

'For goodness sake, Connie,' said Dad. 'Mum's spent ages cooking you spag. bol. as a special treat. Now eat it up at once.'

Connie picked up her forkful of orange worms. She put them in her mouth. Just for a moment they tasted delicious. But then, as her teeth got working and she felt the forkful spread out over her tongue, she thought she felt the worms going wriggle wriggle wriggle.

Connie spat them out in terror.

'Connie!' Dad thundered.

'Connie!' Mum shouted.

Mum didn't often get cross but she was very keen on table manners. And she was very hurt because she'd made the meal specially.

Connie tried to explain, but they just thought she was being naughty. It wasn't fair. Baby Charles and baby Claire spat spoonfuls of food all over the place every single mealtime and no one ever turned a hair. Connie pointed this true fact out to her parents.

'Well, you're *not* a baby,' said Mum. 'Even though you're acting like one now.'

'And you're coming swimming with me on Sundays whether you like it or not,' said Dad.

'But it's so stupid if I don't want to go,' said

Connie, nearly in tears. 'You don't really want to go either, Dad. Not early on Sunday mornings. You'd much sooner have a lie-in.'

'I want you to learn how to swim. It's very important. Every child has to learn. And it's high time you did,' said Dad.

'Why?' said Connie.

'Because you need to learn to swim so you won't ever drown,' said Dad.

'If I stay on dry land then I can't possibly drown,' said Connie. 'But if I go swimming then I could *easily* drown. I very nearly did last Sunday.'

'Don't be so silly, Connie. You just went under for a second, that's all. And I keep telling you, I won't let it happen again.'

'I know you've got a bit scared of swimming because of what happened last time,' said Mum. 'That's *why* we want you to go again. So you can see that there's truly nothing to be scared of. Swimming is great fun. Just give it one more try with Dad. OK?'

It wasn't at all OK with Connie, but she knew she was beaten.

Connie started shivering just at the smell of the swimming-baths. She was shaking so badly she could hardly wriggle into her tight swimming costume. The dolphin on the front was still smiling so she swatted him hard – and punched herself in her own tummy.

Connie had to be dragged to the big pool. Dad held her hand and did his best to be very very patient with her. He helped her down the steps himself, letting her go very slowly. When some other children clambered round impatiently, Dad told them to use the steps at the other side.

'You take your time, Connie,' he said.

They were both shivering by the time Connie eventually got in the water. And then the wave machine was switched on, so Dad hauled Connie out of the water on to the side and let her sit there until the waves had stopped pounding up and down the pool.

'Now, Connie,' said Dad, when they switched the wave machine off at last, 'we'll have a little swimming lesson now. You're going to be a big brave girl, right?'

Wrong. Connie tried, but the moment the turquoise water started lapping round her she couldn't be big or brave. She squealed and shook and shivered. Dad tried pulling her gently along with one hand under her chin and one hand under her tummy, but Connie was so scared of the water she kept arching her back and rearing her head up.

Dad had to give up in the end. He tried sitting Connie on his back so that he could swim along with her.

'You can pretend I'm a great big whale if you like.'

This seemed quite a good idea. Connie clambered on to Dad's back and held tight. Too tight. Dad swam several strokes and the water splashed right in Connie's face.

'Connie! Let go! You're pulling my *hair*!' Dad yelled. 'And get your other arm off my throat, you're strangling me!'

Dad put his feet on the ground. Connie slid off. Into the water. *Under* the water. In the terrifying blue world where she couldn't breathe.

Dad had her up and out of the water in a second, but it was no use. Connie was still crying when they got home.

3 Water Babies

'I'm not going swimming tomorrow,' Connie said on the next Saturday night.

'That's a pity,' said Mum. 'Because we are.'

'We?' said Connie.

'Yep. Claire and Charles and Dad and me,' said Mum.

Connie blinked.

'I think this parent-and-baby session sounds a good idea,' said Mum. 'I want to take the twins. But I can't dangle them in the water together. So I wondered if you'd help me out, Connie? We'll take the babies into the little pool – and Dad can go and have a good swim in the big pool. Yes?'

Connie wasn't sure.

'You like the little pool,' said Mum.

Connie wasn't even sure about that any more. And besides, she had a sneaking suspicion that once they were at the baths Dad would try to get her into the big pool after all.

'You promise I don't have to swim?' she said.

'Not if you don't want to. You just have to hold Claire or Charles in the little pool.'

'I don't think they'll like it,' said Connie.

'They love it in the bath,' said Mum.

Connie snorted. It wasn't as if the babies were super-brave. The least little thing startled them. When Dad played growly bears with them and went 'Grrrr!' they both burst into terrified tears.

'*I* always loved it when you played growly bears with me, Dad,' said Connie.

Mum bought the twins sweet little swimming costumes, red and navy stripes for Claire and green and navy stripes for Charles.

'Would you like a new swimming costume too, Connie?' said Mum. 'Your old dolphin one must be getting a bit small for you now.'

'I don't need a new swimming costume, seeing as I'm never ever going swimming.'

So she wriggled into her tight old costume on Sunday morning. She had to help Mum get the twins undressed and into their new costumes. The swimming-baths had special red plastic changing tables. The twins liked to lie back, kicking their legs.

'They're practising their swimming strokes already,' said the attendant, smiling.

Connie couldn't smile back. The smell and the sound of the baths had made her go all shivery.

'You poor old thing,' said Mum, putting an arm round her. 'You're really frightened, aren't you?'

There were some girls getting changed near by. They were listening. They nudged each other and grinned.

'Of course I'm not frightened,' said Connie fiercely. 'I just think swimming is an incredibly *boring* thing, that's all.'

It came out sounding much ruder than she meant. Mum sighed.

'Really, Connie! Do you have to talk to me in that sulky tone of voice all the time?'

Connie blushed and stuffed Claire's waving pink legs into her small swimming costume. Claire started to whimper and moan because she wanted to stay kicking, stark naked.

'There! You don't want to go swimming, either, do you?' said Connie, picking her up and giving her a cuddle.

Charles started crying too, getting a bit fed up with all this dressing and undressing. Both twins were still yelling when Mum and Connie carried them to the little pool.

'Perhaps this isn't such a good idea after all!' said Mum.

The attendant looked at Connie. 'I thought we agreed before – you're far too big a baby!'

'She's acting as a sort of parent today,' said Mum.

'All right,' the attendant said reluctantly.

Connie held tight to baby Claire. Somehow even the little pool had started to look quite big.

'I don't think Claire wants to go in,' said Connie. 'She keeps crying.'

Charles was crying, too, but when Mum got in the pool and very gently lowered him so that the water lapped round his legs he stopped in mid-squawk. He kicked. He splashed. He smiled.

'Try Claire in the water,' said Mum. 'Charles thinks it's great fun.'

Connie held even tighter to Claire. She put out one foot, dipping the tip of her toe in the little pool.

'Come on,' said Mum. 'Charles, tell your sister that the water's lovely.'

Charles certainly seemed to think so. He wriggled determinedly, doing his best to get away from Mum. He waved his arms and legs in the water. He dipped his head and didn't seem to mind a bit when he got wet. He was smiling from ear to ear.

Claire was fidgeting and fussing, obviously feeling she was missing out.

'Come in the pool, darling,' Mum called.

But Connie couldn't.

In the end Mum had to fetch Dad. He took baby Claire. Mum looked after baby Charles. And Connie sat shivering on the side.

4 Colouring Sharks

'You should see the twins in the pool. It's quite incredible!' said Mum.

'The little pets! They can really *swim*?' said Gran.

'Well . . . not properly, of course. But they bob up and down like ducklings,' said Mum.

'They must look so *sweet*,' said Gran.

'Even when they're in a really niggly mood and nothing else will comfort them, the moment they go in that little swimming-pool they start gurgling happily,' said Mum. She paused. 'Not like *some* people.'

Mum and Gran were talking very quietly, but Connie could still hear every word they were saying. She was drawing a picture of the twins swimming. It had started off a very good picture. Connie was clever at drawing. She drew Claire and Charles looking very cute in their stripy swimming costumes.

Mum and Gran had said it was a beautiful picture. But then they'd sat on the sofa together and went on and on and *on* about the twins and swimming.

Connie suddenly drew a great big enormous shark in the swimming-pool with the twins. The shark had a great big enormous mouth glittering with sharp teeth. It was swimming very near the twins. It looked as if it was about to have a delicious baby-snack for breakfast.

'Poor Connie! So this being scared of swimming has developed into a real phobia?' said Gran.

Connie didn't know exactly what a phobia was, but it sounded feeble and pathetic and babyish. She *felt* feeble and pathetic and babyish. She bent her head over her drawing. There was suddenly a spot of real water puddling the swimming-pool picture.

'Connie?' said Mum. 'Are you all right?'

'Mmm,' said Connie.

'I've just been talking things over with Gran,' said Mum.

'That's right, dear,' said Gran. 'I've been telling your mum I'd love it if you came round to visit me on Sunday mornings. Would you like that, Connie? You can bring all your bits and pieces to play with – and maybe you'll draw me some lovely pictures to pin up in my kitchen. Let's see your picture of the twins swimming. Have you finished it?'

'Not quite,' said Connie quickly. She took her blue felt tip and scribbled hurriedly over the great big enormous shark.

'Connie, don't do it like that! You'll go over all the lines,' said Mum.

'I'm just colouring in the water,' said Connie.

The shark simply wouldn't go away, no matter how hard she coloured over him.

'Let's see,' said Gran, getting up.

'Whoops,' said Connie. 'Oh dear, yes, I've spoilt it.'

She tore the page out of her drawing book and crumpled it up in her fist.

'Oh, Connie!' said Gran. 'What a shame!'

'Never mind, Gran. I'll draw you another one next Sunday,' said Connie.

Next Sunday she did draw Gran a picture. She drew herself, on dry land.

'It's a *lovely* picture, dear!' said Gran, and she pinned it up on the kitchen wall.

Then Connie drew a picture of Gran.

'Why have you drawn all those dark bits on my forehead?' Gran said. 'I look as if I've got a dirty face.'

'That's all the wrinkles,' said Connie.

'Oh dear,' said Gran, and she sighed.

'Aren't you going to pin that picture up too?' said Connie.

'Yes, of course, dear,' said Gran, looking at her face in the shiny kettle, and sighing again. 'How about doing a portrait of Grandpa now?'

Grandpa wasn't very well. He spent a lot of his time having a little doze. He dozed all the time Connie was drawing his portrait. Connie went to show Gran the finished picture.

'I wish you hadn't drawn him with his mouth open,' said Gran, but she pinned that picture up too.

Connie wanted to watch television now but Gran's set was very old and kept twitching. Her video recorder hadn't worked properly for ages either.

'The hire firm is replacing them on Monday,' said Gran, and her face creased into a whole new set of wrinkles.

'What's the matter, Gran?' said Connie.

'Nothing, nothing. Tell you what – you help me peel the vegetables for lunch and then I'll read to you, eh?'

Connie wasn't too thrilled about this idea. Gran had a whole shelf of children's story-books but they were all very long and old-fashioned. Gran wasn't very good at reading aloud either, not a patch on the people who read on Connie's collection of story-tapes. But Connie smiled and acted pleased. She was trying to be good for once because she was fed up with Mum and Dad thinking her bad.

But Gran picked the worst possible book. It was called *The Water Babies*.

'I don't want that book!' said Connie.

'It's a lovely book, dear, all about this little boy Tom who's a chimney sweep and then he becomes a water baby. Look, it's got beautiful pictures.'

Connie wouldn't look, Connie wouldn't listen. When Mum and Dad and the twins came to fetch her, Gran whispered to Mum that Connie had been a 'bit of a madam'.

Connie felt this was most unfair. She felt cross for the rest of Sunday. But she cheered up at school on Monday. She sat next to her best friend Karen. Karen had a baby sister called Susie, who screamed a lot. Karen drew a silly picture of Susie on the back of her school jotter. Connie and Karen got the giggles.

Connie was still smiling when she met up with Mum at the school gate.

'You look in a good mood for once,' said Mum. 'Come on, we're in a hurry. I've got to take the twins to be weighed at the baby clinic.'

'The baby clinic?' said Connie. 'Will Nurse Meade be there?'

'She should be,' said Mum.

'Great!' said Connie. 'She's *magic*.'

5 Giant Gerbil

'Hello, Nurse Meade! Remember me?' said Connie, running up to Nurse Meade.

'Of course I remember you, Connie,' Nurse Meade laughed, and all the little blue glass beads on the ends of her plaits twinkled.

'You've still got all your pretty plaits,' said Connie.

'With my special blue glass beads,' said Nurse Meade, and she winked at Connie.

Connie winked back. She wasn't very good at winking. She had to crease up half of her face in the process.

'Connie, are you making faces at Nurse Meade?' said Mum, shocked.

'She's just being friendly. We're special friends, Connie and me,' said Nurse Meade. 'How about helping me weigh your little brother and sister then, Connie? Off with their nappies and into the scales.'

They weighed Claire first. She disgraced herself by doing a little wee in the scales. Mum got all embarrassed but Nurse Meade only laughed.

Then they weighed Charles. He wasn't going to let Claire outdo him. He did a little wee too. This time Nurse Meade had to dodge out of the way! She laughed even more. Connie laughed so much she had to clutch her sides and stagger.

'I'm going to wear my swimming costume next time I weigh these two,' said Nurse Meade.

Connie stopped laughing. Nurse Meade looked thoughtful. Mum was busy mopping Claire and Charles and getting them dressed.

'Lots of people take their babies swimming

now,' said Nurse Meade, cleaning her scales.

'Yes, I take Claire and Charles,' said Mum, trying to sound casual.

'And do they like it?' asked Nurse Meade, washing her hands.

'They love it,' said Mum. She glanced worriedly at Connie.

Nurse Meade was watching Connie carefully too.

'Do you like swimming, Connie?' asked Nurse Meade.

'No. I hate it,' said Connie.

'Is that so?' said Nurse Meade. 'Hey, your hair's grown quite a bit since I last saw you. Do you ever wear it in little plaits like me?'

'They're too fiddly for me to fix myself – and Mum's always too busy,' said Connie. 'I loved it when you gave me a little plait, Nurse Meade.'

'Do you want me to give you just one little plait now?' asked Nurse Meade.

'Yes, please!'

'With a couple of my blue glass beads to keep it in place?' asked Nurse Meade. She took two out of the pocket of her blue dress and held them up to the light. They sparkled a deep bright blue. A familiar frightening colour.

Connie suddenly shivered.

'What's up, Connie? You loved my beads last time,' Nurse Meade said gently.

'Yes, but . . . they're swimming-pool blue. And I hate that colour now.' Connie hesitated. Nurse Meade started plaiting a lock of her hair. 'I'm a little bit scared of swimming, actually,' Connie mumbled.

'Is that so?' said Nurse Meade, still plaiting, as if it was no big deal at all. 'Ah well. We're all scared of something.'

'Dad gets cross with me. And Mum's ever so tactful but she really thinks I'm a baby. And Gran says I've got a phobia,' said Connie.

'I get the picture,' said Nurse Meade. 'Well, I wouldn't worry about it too much, Connie. I have a feeling things will somehow sort themselves out.' She finished the plait, holding it together with her finger and thumb. 'I can find a bit of ribbon for you if you really don't want to wear my blue beads.'

Nurse Meade looked at Connie. Connie looked back at Nurse Meade.

'A ribbon wouldn't be anywhere near as . . . magic,' said Nurse Meade.

'I'd like the blue beads after all, please,' said Connie.

Nurse Meade twisted them into place. Connie couldn't see them when she looked straight ahead but when she turned her head quickly she saw a little blue spark bob up over her ear. Connie still didn't like being reminded of swimming-pools – but the beads were beautiful.

'I see Nurse Meade's given you some of her beads again,' said Mum.

'Yes. They're magic,' said Connie, very hopefully indeed.

'Were you talking about being scared of swimming to Nurse Meade?' said Mum on their way home from the clinic.

'Mmm,' said Connie, not wanting to talk about it now.

'I know you're very scared and it must be horrible for you.' Mum insisted on talking about it. 'I do understand, darling. But you must see that there's really nothing to be scared

of, not in the baby pool.'

'And boring old baby Charles and baby Claire bob up and down in it like little ducks. Why can't you all just shut up about it?'

Mum was now very cross indeed so when they got home Connie stomped off by herself into the back garden. She twiddled the two blue beads on her new plait. She was sick of Mum. She wished for two new twin mums*. But the magic didn't seem to work this time. No new mums appeared though Connie looked all around hopefully. She twiddled the beads once more. 'Come on, you're meant to be magic!'

'Who are you talking to?' said a voice over the fence.

It was Gerald, the big boy next door. He certainly wasn't magic, but Connie liked him all the same.

'Come on, my little beauties,' muttered Gerald.

'Who are *you* talking to, Gerald?' asked Connie.

'My gerbils have had babies. Want to see them?'

'Oooh yes,' said Connie.

The baby gerbils were very cute indeed. They were more like toddler gerbils,

* see *Twin Trouble*

bright-eyed and alert, with fluffy coats and long tickly tails.

'They're lovely,' said Connie, enchanted. 'Let me hold one, please.'

'Well, be careful. Don't drop it!'

'Of course I won't.' Connie held her hands out over the fence and Gerald gently dropped a soft little baby gerbil into her palm.

'Oooh, it's so *sweet*!' Connie whispered.

'You can have one if you promise to look after it properly,' said Gerald.

'I don't think my mum would let me. I don't think she likes gerbils. She's mad. They're the cutest little animals ever. But ever so tickly!' The gerbil was running up her arm and into the tunnel of her T-shirt sleeve. 'Hey, come back!' said Connie, giggling. 'Gerald, it's escaping!'

Gerald sighed. 'I told you to hold on to it. Wait a minute. I'll have to secure the others before I can help.'

Connie's gerbil was whizzing down her leg and was off up the lawn before she could stop it.

'Come back, little gerbil!' Connie called, running.

The gerbil scampered across the patio and in through the open back door. There was a sudden scream. A very loud frantic s-c-r-e-a-m.

'That's Mum,' said Connie, running harder.

Mum was in the kitchen, climbing right up the cupboards, her head nearly banging the ceiling. She was yelling her head off.

The gerbil was on the tiled floor, peering up at Mum. It didn't look such a baby now. In fact it seemed very big for an adult gerbil. It seemed to be growing rapidly. It was a good cat-size now, with huge pointed teeth and an immense quivery tail.

'Run!' Mum shouted desperately to Connie.

The gerbil heard the word 'run' and decided to obey. It went charging across the kitchen, its claws gouging great tracks across the floor. It grew at every stride. It skittered to a halt at the kitchen unit. It could almost get its huge head over the edge.

'Aaaah!' Mum yelled hysterically, hopping up and down.

'Calm down, Mum,' said Connie cheerily. 'I know you're very scared. It must be horrible for you. I do understand, honest. But you must see that there's really nothing to be scared of. It's only a little baby gerbil!'

As soon as Connie spoke the gerbil started shrinking.

'Come here, little gerbil,' said Connie, bending to pick it up. The gerbil shrivelled right back to its meek mild self, far smaller than Connie's hand.

'See?' said Connie, holding it up to show Mum.

'Take it away,' Mum whispered hoarsely.

Connie did as she was told. Then she went back to the kitchen and helped Mum down from the cupboard. Mum was still shaking like a jelly.

'Nothing to be scared of now, Mum,' said Connie reassuringly.

'Oh, Connie! You

were so *brave*,' said Mum. 'The bravest girl in all the world.'

6 Exploding Video

Gerald said the baby gerbil could be Connie's special pet, even though it would have to live in a cage in Gerald's back garden. She told everybody at school about George Gerbil.

It was art first lesson so Connie drew a portrait of George. She drew him looking rather big and fierce, almost filling up the entire sheet of paper. Then right at the top Connie drew Mum shrieking and climbing up the kitchen cupboards.

'That's very good, Connie,' said Miss Peters. 'But I think you've got the proportions all wrong. You've made your gerbil look much too big.'

'He did look as big as that, Miss Peters,' said Connie. 'Mum thought he did too!'

Connie wrote about George Gerbil in the English lesson and she chose gerbils as the animal for her nature project.

'You seem to have a one-track mind today, Connie,' said Miss Peters. 'Well, it's PE last lesson. I suppose you're going to run as fast as a gerbil, right?'

'Maybe,' said Connie, laughing.

She wasn't very good at running. Or jumping or catching a ball. But it didn't really matter, because Connie's best friend Karen wasn't very good either. They were generally partners and puffed along together. Today Connie and Karen were nearly last in the race.

'Slowcoaches!' said Angela. 'Honestly, you two, you're hopeless.'

Angela had come first, even beating the boys.

'Who wants to run like *you*?' said Connie.

Angela did ballet and was always sticking her feet out sideways. Connie did a funny imitation and everyone laughed.

'Now then, Connie,' said Miss Peters. 'Don't be silly, or I'll make you run the race all over again.'

'Oh, Miss Peters! I hate running,' said Connie.

'I know. Ah well, I don't suppose you can be good at everything. And maybe you'll come into your own next term.'

'What are we doing next term, Miss Peters?' Karen asked.

'It's a special treat,' said Miss Peters.

'Is it dancing?' Angela asked hopefully.

'Yuck! I hope not!' said Connie.

'No, it's not dancing. We're going to go swimming.'

'Swimming!' said everyone excitedly.

Everyone but Connie.

'Swimming!' she whispered, appalled.

'Yes, we've fixed it all up with the local swimming-pool. Our class can go once a week – in the big pool too!'

Connie closed her eyes. That terrible blue watery world seemed to be swirling all around her. What was she going to do now? Could she manage a terrible cold/stomach ache/headache every single swimming lesson? It might work once or twice, but Miss Peters was no fool.

'Oh help,' Connie mumbled.

'What's up, Connie?' said Karen.

'Nothing,' said Connie quickly.

'It's great about swimming, isn't it?' said Karen. 'Heaps better than boring old PE. You go swimming with your dad, don't you?'

'I . . . used to,' said Connie. 'We haven't gone much recently.'

Connie started to feel sick. She could see their whole class at the swimming-baths. Everyone showing off and teasing each other. She saw herself, shivering, scared, screaming. She'd never ever ever be able to live it down.

She was still feeling sick when she came out of school. Gran had come to meet Connie.

'Hello, dear. What's the matter? What's happened? You look dreadful, Connie!'

'It's nothing, Gran,' said Connie, hurrying to get away from all the other children.

Gran was in a hurry too, not wanting to miss her favourite quiz programme on television.

'Why don't you set your new video so that it records it while you're out?' said Connie.

'Oh, I . . . I didn't think of that,' said Gran, sounding odd. 'Come on, then, dear.' They were passing the ice-cream van. 'I think we can make time for an ice-cream,' said Gran. 'Would you like a giant ninety-nine with strawberry sauce?'

Normally Connie would say YES, PLEASE. But she was still feeling so sick about swimming that she simply shook her head.

Gran stared at her.

'Connie, there's something *really* the matter, isn't there?' Gran put her arm round Connie and held her close.

'Tell me what it is, darling,' said Gran.

Connie screwed up her face. Her eyes were stinging and she was terribly scared she might cry. She took Gran's hand and hurried her down the street and round the corner. Then she blurted it out.

'Miss Peters said we've got to go swimming with the school next term,' she wailed.

Gran looked at her blankly.

'But that's good, isn't it, dear? You've got

yourself in a silly state about going swimming with Mummy and Daddy. Now you can go with all your friends and learn properly.'

'Oh, Gran! You don't understand. I *can't* go swimming. I'm *scared*!'

'But it's so silly to be scared, Connie,' said Gran, sighing. 'I don't know. I can't understand the way you children are brought up nowadays. Your mum shouldn't give in to you so. We just had to put up with things when we were kiddies. Nobody bothered to ask whether we were scared or not. We just had to do as we were told.'

Connie was extremely annoyed with Gran.

Gran hurried along the road. Connie trailed after her, twiddling the blue beads on her plait. As she went into Gran's house they gave a little blue spark.

Gran went into her living-room – and gave a shriek. Connie rushed in after her.

'Look!' said Gran, pointing with a shaking finger.

'Wow!' said Connie.

The new television and video recorder were hissing and buzzing and crackling ominously, lightning forks of electricity shooting off in all directions. They were covered with hundreds of knobs and buttons, all of them lighting up and flashing like Christmas-tree lights. There were clocks and time switches all over the place, numbers blurring they were going so fast. Different programmes danced across the screen of the television set, while the video recorder opened up all by itself and sucked in Gran's favourite video, *The Sound of Music*. It chewed it all up in a split second and spat it out again with a very rude electronic burp.

'Oh my goodness!' Gran wailed. 'I'll have to phone the television man again! I don't know what to do. He's shown me how to work it twice but I can't get the hang of it at all – and the instruction booklet is written in a completely foreign language. Grandpa's too old to work it out – and I'm so useless with modern machines. They scare me so.'

Gran cowered away from the television, squealing as an entire firework display shot out of the set and circled the ceiling.

'It's OK, Gran,' said Connie cheerily. 'It's a bit silly to be scared of a television, but never mind. I don't know. I can't understand the way you grown-ups feel about machines. We children don't act so daft. It's really easy-peasy. Look!'

She sauntered up to the television and video and pressed a button. They instantly subsided. Connie inserted *The Sound of Music* and pressed another button. It rewound, as good as new. Then Connie selected the right channel and pressed one more button. Gran's quiz programme came on to the screen.

'There we are, Gran. I'll set your video so that it records it automatically for you in future, OK?'

'Oh, Connie! You clever clever clever little girl,' said Gran, clapping her hands.

And Grandpa woke up at last and gave Connie a big smile.

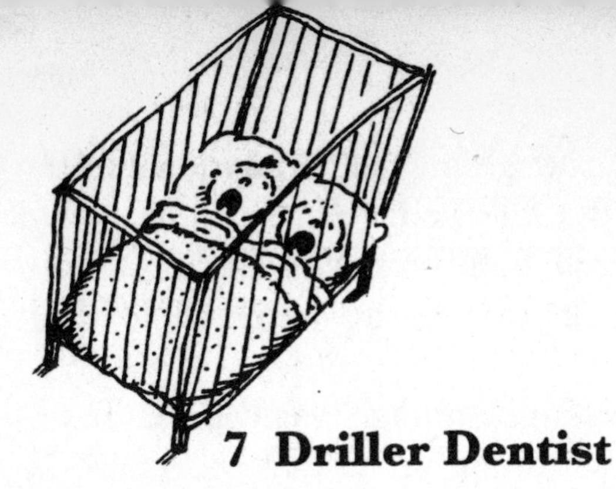

7 Driller Dentist

Connie woke up with a start, her arms and legs flailing. She pushed back her duvet, gasping for air – and then sighed with relief. She was safe in her own dry bed – not down in the depths of that cold blue pool.

She glanced at her Little Mermaid alarm clock (oh dear, even that seemed sinister nowadays!) to see if it was time to get up.

'Mum! Dad! We've slept in,' Connie called, jumping out of bed.

Mum and Dad came staggering out of their bedroom, their eyes all peepy and their hair sticking up on end.

'Claire and Charles cried half the night!' Mum said. 'I had to give them another feed at four o'clock this morning – and *still* they didn't settle.'

The twins woke up at the sound of their names and started wailing.

'Oh no!' said Mum, staggering down to the kitchen to put the kettle on. 'Connie, you'd better share the bathroom with Dad. You have a very quick in-and-out bath while Dad shaves.'

'You haven't got enough water in that bath,' said Dad, his mouth all sideways because he was shaving.

'It's fine,' said Connie, having a quick swish.

'Don't be silly – it's only a couple of centimetres! You can't wash in that,' said Dad, reaching out to turn the bath taps back on.

'I don't want it any deeper!' Connie yelled.

'Oh, for goodness sake! You're not scared of the *bath* now, are you? This is ridiculous, Connie. You're not a *baby*. You've got to conquer this stupid fear or you'll end up completely loopy – and you'll drive us all daft as well. Aaaaah!'

It was Dad who sounded daft, screeching like that. He'd concentrated too much on Connie and not enough on his shaving.

Connie hunched up in her shallow bath, twisting her little plait and twiddling the blue beads for all she was worth.

'What's going on? Are you all right?' said Mum, putting her head round the door.

'No, I'm not! I've cut myself,' said Dad, trying to staunch the wound with a little wad of toilet paper.

'Well, hurry up out the way and let Connie clean her teeth in the basin. I've just noticed a ring round the date on the calendar downstairs. Connie's got to go to the dentist for her check-up. It's a nine o'clock appointment – so you'll have to step on it. You can both have breakfast afterwards,' said Mum.

'What? What are you on about? *I* can't take Connie to the dentist. I've got to go to work.'

'I'm sorry, you'll just have to be late for work for once. I can't possibly take Connie in time.'

'But you know I can't . . . ' said Dad, looking strange.

Mum sighed. 'Look, I'd normally take Connie, you know that. But she simply can't miss her appointment. Not like *some* people.' Mum sounded a bit strange too.

Dad still acted strange as he was driving Connie to the dentist. His hands were all shaky as he clutched the wheel of the car, as if he was very cold – and yet he had little beads of sweat on his forehead. His face twitched every now and then, and the little wad of toilet paper stuck to his shaving cut twitched too.

'Dad, are you all right?' said Connie.

'Yes, of course I am,' said Dad. But his voice was all high and wavery – almost as if he was *scared.*

'You've still got toilet paper stuck to your face, Dad,' said Connie, as they drew up outside the dental surgery.

Dad swatted it away from his chin. He switched off the ignition. He gave Connie a very weird wild smile.

'Off you go then, Connie. I'll just wait for you in the car,' he said.

Connie stared at Dad. 'But you have to come in too, Dad. You have to sign all the forms and stuff.'

'Oh dear. Right.'

He seemed to have great difficulty getting out of the car. He wavered all over the place going up the pathway to the surgery door.

'I think you might have really hurt yourself shaving. Maybe you've got tetanus or something, from the cut?'

'Don't be silly, Connie,' Dad murmured, and then he staggered into the surgery.

Connie followed him and looked round in astonishment. It seemed to have changed a great deal since she was last there six months ago. The waiting-room was terribly cold and all the pictures were missing from the walls. All the magazines and toys had been cleared away. There were just horrible leaflets with pictures of people with bleeding mouths and crumbling teeth.

Connie was great friends with the pretty young receptionist – but she didn't seem to be around today. There was a fierce frowny woman in her place in a crackly white uniform, wearing a mask and rubber gloves.

She pointed straight at Dad. 'Aha! You're the man who's missed all his appointments!'

'I'm sorry,' Dad said – and then a terrible, achingly loud drilling sound started up in the next room. It was so ear-splitting that the wall vibrated and Connie was jiggled up and down. Dad threw himself to the floor, his hands over his mouth, and whimpered. Then the drill suddenly stopped and they heard footsteps outside.

Someone burst into the waiting-room, a huge terrifying white figure in cap and gown. He was holding huge steel pointed instruments in either hand and was chuckling manically behind his white mask.

Dad took one look at him and shrieked.

But Connie smiled. 'What's up, Dad? You're not scared of the dentist, are you? This is ridiculous. You're not a baby. You've got to conquer this stupid fear or you'll end up completely loopy! There's nothing at all to be scared of.'

'Of course there's nothing to be scared of, Connie,' said the dentist – and he shrank back to his usual jolly self. His terrifying steel instruments vanished, happy music played in the prettily decorated waiting-room, and the young receptionist waved at Connie.

'Hi there, Connie. Are you here for your six-monthly examination?' She looked at Dad, who was standing up sheepishly. 'Goodness! You've brought your dad with you today. It's a *very* long time since we've seen you. Would you like an appointment too?'

'I suppose so,' Dad said. 'I tell you what. I'll have my teeth examined if Connie stands beside me and holds my hand tight!'

8 Mermaid Magic

'Connie, your hair's getting to look like a little floor mop!' said Mum, ruffling Connie's unruly hair. 'I must wash it for you tonight.'

'Oh no, Mum!' said Connie, shaking her head vigorously.

Mum looked really worried. 'Oh, Connie – this being fussed about water is getting right out of hand. You've *got* to have your hair washed, darling.'

'I'm not *scared*, Mum,' said Connie. 'I just don't want to lose my little plait with the blue glass beads.'

'Oh, the one Nurse Meade did for you. Yes, it does look cute. Well, I'll have a go at plaiting your hair after I've washed it, though I don't know how Nurse Meade twiddles those little beads into place.'

'They twiddle in a very special way, Mum,' said Connie. 'Let me keep my hair

like this a bit longer, please!'

Mum got as far as fetching the shampoo – but then Charles spat out his dummy and started crying hard. By the time both twins were fast asleep Mum flopped into her armchair and watched the television, too tired to start shampooing. Connie skipped off to bed that night with her plait still in place, the blue beads gently jingling.

She fingered her plait fondly as she cuddled down to sleep – and when she started dreaming she chinked the two blue beads together so that they sparked bright blue in the dark of Connie's bedroom.

The blue seeped into Connie's dreams. She found herself floundering in a vast pool of water. It was dragging her down, right underneath, and she was choking and struggling – but then someone caught hold of her round her waist and lifted her up and out of the water, her head bursting free into sudden sunlight. She wasn't in a pool at all, she was at a strange new seaside, with the blue waves sparkling in the sunlight.

Connie rose up out of the waves, through the waves, *on to* the waves, skimming along their surface as if she were riding a surfboard. The hands were still around her waist, holding her gently but firmly, steering her along, swooping her up on the crest of each wave, foam dancing about her ankles.

It was someone who looked surprisingly familiar, black beaded plaits flying in the breeze, all the glass beads as sparkling blue as the sea itself. This someone wasn't wearing a blue uniform. She wasn't wearing any sort of dress at all, and from her waist downwards she was all shimmering tail, flickering gracefully as they leapt in and out of the water.

'You're a mermaid!' said Connie.

She looked down at her own legs again, wondering if she'd turned into a mermaid too. No, her two legs were still there, sometimes leaping right out of the water with neat pointed toes, other times kicking purposefully through the waves.

'I'm swimming!' said Connie.

The mermaid laughed, and a whole school of dolphins with smiley faces whistled and squeaked in a friendly way at Connie. They all skimmed the surface of the sea together and then dived downwards, disappearing.

'Oh, come back, little dolphins!' cried Connie. 'Where have you gone?'

She tried to peer through the water beneath her. She saw strange flowers and coral rocks and stripy fish and her new dolphin friends playing follow-my-leader.

'Can we go down there too?' Connie said.

The mermaid smiled again and then Connie found herself diving down through the water into a new brighter, bluer world and she could breathe easily and swim almost as fast as the dolphins and she chased them all around the sea garden until she was tired, and then she sat on a rock with the mermaid, who combed her hair with a mother-of-pearl comb and then plaited it and started to fix the two blue beads back into place – but they slipped from her fingers and spiralled downwards through the blue sea, down and down into the dark …

And then Connie woke up, and it was light and morning. She put her hands on to her hair. It was wet – as if she'd really been swimming in the sea. She felt for her plait, but it was just a little tangled lock, fast unravelling. The blue beads were gone.

Connie lay quietly, thinking about her dream. She thought about swimming. Somehow it didn't seem quite such a scary idea now.

She jumped out of bed and ran into her parents' room.

'Hey, Mum, Dad! It's Sunday. Are you going swimming with the twins?'

'I think I'll give it a miss today,' Mum mumbled sleepily from under the duvet. 'They both woke up in the night and needed feeding. We're all too tired this morning.'

'I'm not a bit tired. And I'd like to go swimming. Will you take me, Dad? Please?'

'You want to go *swimming*, Connie?' said Dad, sitting bolt upright.

'Yes, please.'

'But . . . ' said Dad. 'I thought . . . '

'Just take her!' Mum mumbled.

So Dad stumbled out of bed and took Connie swimming. Connie wasn't quite so sure this was a good idea when they went into the swimming-baths. She hesitated at the door, her lip trembling.

Dad didn't say anything at all – but he gave her a quick hug.

Connie knew he'd take her straight home if that was what she really wanted. But she wanted to swim. So she'd jolly well have to give it a go, even if she was scared after all. Very, very scared.

She stomped off into the ladies' changing-room, wishing like anything that she still had her blue beads to twiddle. And there right in front of her was a flash of blue! It was Nurse Meade, in a bright blue swimming costume to match her magic beads.

'Hey there, Connie!' she called.

'Nurse Meade!' said Connie. 'Oh, how super! Have you come for a swim?'

'I thought it seemed a good idea,' said Nurse Meade. 'So you've come for a swim too, Connie?'

'Yes. I thought it seemed a good idea too,' said Connie, hurriedly changing into her swimming costume.

The dolphin on the front was smiling all over his face.

'He's OK,' said Connie, tickling him under

his chin. 'He knows how to swim.'

'I'll show you how to swim if you like, Connie,' said Nurse Meade, taking her hand.

They were out of the changing-rooms before Dad. The little learner pool was still being used for the babies.

'I guess it's the big pool,' said Connie, and she hung back a little.

'Getting in is the worst bit,' said Nurse Meade. 'Let's keep holding hands as we go down the steps.'

They did just that – and somehow it wasn't quite so bad, even when the water was lapping right up around Connie's neck.

'I'll take you for a little swim, shall I?' said Nurse Meade.

She held Connie gently but firmly round her waist and pulled her along through the water. Connie held her head up high and let her feet waft up off the bottom of the pool.

'Kick those feet a little,' said Nurse Meade.

Connie kicked.

'And paddle your hands through the water,' said Nurse Meade.

Connie paddled.

'There! You're swimming!'

'Only sort of,' Connie gasped.

The water washed over her chin and splashed her face but even that wasn't so bad now. Nurse Meade showed her how to dip her face right into the water and blow bubbles just like a little fish. Connie dipped and blew. Soon she dared bend her knees and duck right down. She didn't mind a bit. She wasn't scared any more!

Dad was sitting on the side of the pool, staring.

'Watch me, Dad,' Connie called. 'Let's do some more swimming, Nurse Meade.'

Nurse Meade pulled her carefully along while Connie paddled with her hands and kicked with her feet. Once the water splashed right up so that she spluttered, but she blew bubbles through it and went on paddling and kicking.

'Shall I let go just for a second?' said Nurse Meade.

Connie thought about it – and then nodded.

'Keep swimming, Connie,' said Nurse Meade, taking her hands away.

So Connie paddled and kicked as hard as she could – and for two whole strokes she was swimming all by herself. Then Nurse Meade clasped her round the waist again, keeping her safe.

'Well done, Connie!' she said.

'Well done, Connie!' said Dad, jumping into the water, absolutely thrilled.

'I can swim. I can really swim! Hey, let's go swimming every single Sunday, Dad, and then I'll be able to swim a whole length by the time we go swimming with the school,' said Connie. 'Will you come too, Nurse Meade?'

'Maybe once or twice,' said Nurse Meade.

She smiled at Connie and Connie smiled back. When they were getting dressed after their swim, Nurse Meade pulled on shiny green leggings and pointy green pearlised boots. It looked almost as if she had a real mermaid's tail . . .

TWIN TROUBLE

Jacqueline Wilson

'Nobody asked me whether I wanted the twins. I'm part of the family aren't I? You don't know what it's like for me. I wish there was some way I could make you understand.

Eight-year-old Connie is in despair. Then Nurse Meade arrives with her long black hair twisted into little plaits fastened with tiny blue glass beads.

When Connie twiddles with the two blue beads the nurse has given her, something magical begins to happen . . .

A hilarious and comforting story about the arrival of twins in the family.